I Think I Can!
A Search-and-Find Book

by
Terrance Crawford

**Can you find all
the toy trains?**

illustrated by
Jannie Ho

GROSSET & DUNLAP
An imprint of Penguin Random House LLC, New York

First published in the United States of America by Grosset & Dunlap, an imprint of Penguin Random House LLC, New York, 2023

Copyright © 2023 by Penguin Random House LLC

Based on the book THE LITTLE ENGINE THAT COULD (The Complete, Original Edition) by Watty Piper, illustrated by George & Doris Hauman, © Penguin Random House LLC.
The Little Engine That Could®, I Think I Can®, and all related titles, logos, and characters are trademarks of Penguin Random House LLC. All rights reserved.

Penguin supports copyright. Copyright fuels creativity, encourages diverse voices, promotes free speech, and creates a vibrant culture.
Thank you for buying an authorized edition of this book and for complying with copyright laws by not reproducing, scanning, or distributing any part
of it in any form without permission. You are supporting writers and allowing Penguin to continue to publish books for every reader.

GROSSET & DUNLAP is a registered trademark of Penguin Random House LLC.

Visit us online at penguinrandomhouse.com.

Manufactured in China

ISBN 9780593658581   10 9 8 7 6 5 4 3 2 1 HH

Design by Mary Claire Cruz

Huff Huff, Puff Puff!

The Little Blue Engine was chug-chug-chugging along, huffing and puffing her way to find the clown, the elephant, the airplane, the giraffe, the dolls, the bears, and the monkey! She can't wait to spend the day with her friends! Help Little Engine find:

the Little Engine That Could herself!

the elephant

the monkey

the giraffe

the airplane

the two bears

the clown

the two dolls

The City

The Little Blue Engine and her friends rumble into the first stop on their list—the city! Can you help the friends find everything on their list in all the hustle and bustle?

four cats

five pretzels

three dogs

four taxicabs

two fire hydrants

three pigeons

three hot-dog carts

two traffic lights

The Park

The Little Blue Engine huffs and puffs her way to their next stop—the park! The Little Blue Engine and her friends need your help to find:

seven pine trees

three blue flowers

four birds

three picnic baskets

a deer

three clouds in the shape of:

a puppy

a rabbit

a flower

two park benches

two chipmunks

The Beach

Hope you brought your sunblock for the next stop on our trip—the beach! Take a quick dip and help the Little Blue Engine find:

three beach balls

two beach towels

four beach umbrellas

six pairs of sunglasses

three seagulls

a hot dog

four seashells

three starfish

a sandcastle

The Farm

The Little Blue Engine can hear the cows mooing and the horses neighing as they arrive at the next stop on their list— the farm! Don't let the sheep pull the wool over your eyes! Help the Little Blue Engine and her friends find:

two sheep

three bales of hay

a rooster

four pigs

three cows

a tractor

two horses

six eggs

Clown Town

The Little Blue Engine and her friends always put on a happy face when they pull into their next stop—Clown Town! Have a laugh while you help find:

three blue noses

six juggling pins

four rabbits

five large shoes

two green bow ties

three polka-dot hats

a circus tent

eight balloons

The Marketplace

Phew! The Little Blue Engine and her friends are starting to get hungry. Luckily, they know just the place to stop—the marketplace! As they refuel, help them find:

five apples

three doughnuts

two eggplants

a pumpkin

two ice-cream cones

three potatoes

two sunflowers

four slices of pie

four bananas

FRESH FRUIT

SALE
Jam $6
CHEESE $10
PIE $12

The Forest

There sure are a lot of trees at our next stop—the forest! Try not to get stumped while you help the Little Blue Engine and her friends find:

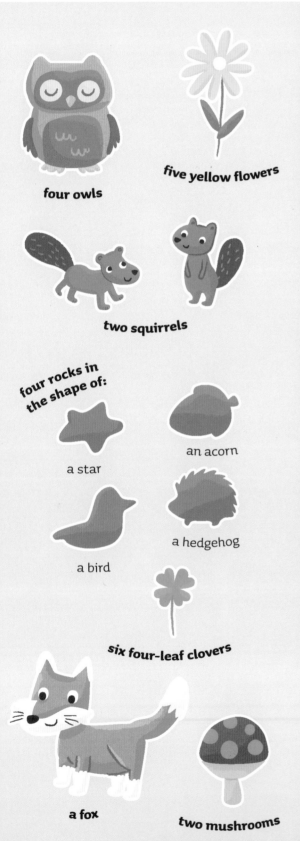

four owls

five yellow flowers

two squirrels

four rocks in the shape of:

a star

an acorn

a bird

a hedgehog

six four-leaf clovers

a fox

two mushrooms

The Cave

Next stop: the cave! Hey, who turned out the lights?! See if you can help the Little Blue Engine find:

Bigfoot

three bats

two pairs of mysterious eyes

a bear

two fossils

two treasure chests

three spiders

two beetles

The River

The next stop on the list brings the Little Blue Engine and her friends down by the river! Go with the flow and help the Little Blue Engine find:

eight dark brown twigs

seven stones

two beavers

three dragonflies

four pink fish

two tree stumps

three frogs

a turtle

The Ice Cap

Everyone has to bundle up for the next stop on the list—an ice cap! Stay chill and help the Little Blue Engine and her friends find:

a polar bear

three pairs of skis

ten snowflakes

a snowboar...

three scarves

two hot cocoas

two orange winter hats

three pairs of red mittens

Aquarium

The Little Blue Engine and all her friends have arrived at their next stop—the aquarium! See what you can see and help the Little Blue Engine and her friends find:

three starfish

four octopuses

a whale

a diver

two dolphins

two lobsters

three puffer fish

three manatees

four mermaids

The Tropical Island

The day is winding down! Take in the sights at the tropical island! Soak up the sun while you help the Little Blue Engine and her friends find the things on their list:

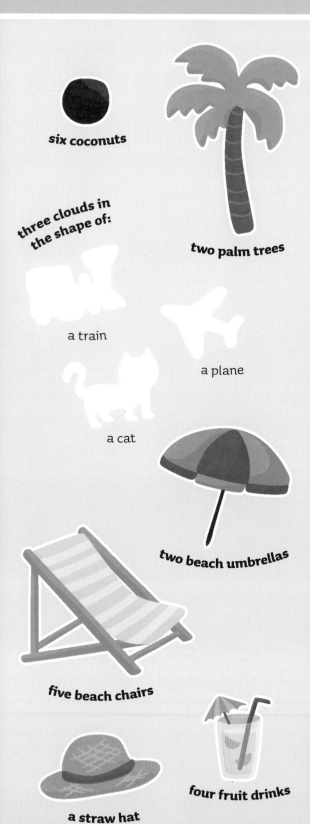

six coconuts

two palm trees

three clouds in the shape of:

a train

a plane

a cat

two beach umbrellas

five beach chairs

a straw hat

four fruit drinks

Stargazing

The sun went down, and the clown, the elephant, the bears, the dolls, the giraffe, the airplane, and the monkey can't remember the last time they had this much fun! The Little Blue Engine can't wait for their next adventure! Look through the night sky and help Little Engine find:

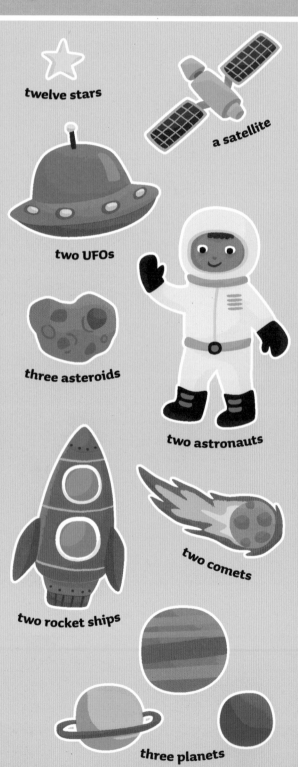

twelve stars

a satellite

two UFOs

three asteroids

two astronauts

two rocket ships

two comets

three planets

Answer Key

Did you spot the **toy train** in every puzzle, too?